My Great Ocean Road Adventure Belongs to:

____

Look out for Nelly The Wombat
.....she likes to hide!

For Harry and for Gilbert

Harry loves 'writing' letters to his Grandparents known as Mac and Pa.
'My Great Ocean Road Adventure' is another letter Harry wishes to
share with you as part of the 'My Adventure Series'.

This series has been created to promote Australia.
More important however, it is to encourage children to have a sense of fun and imagination.
We also hope that children will be encouraged to write a letter....and post it!

Look out for further books in this series:
My Melbourne Adventure
My Sydney Adventure
My Aussie Bush Adventure
My Aussie Ocean Adventure
My Phillip Island Adventure
My Mornington Peninsula Adventure
My Warburton Adventure
My Adventure Books CD

Also by Rothwell Publishing:
The Big Hungry Tree

9 Clarke Avenue Warburton, Victoria, Australia, 3799
www.rothwellpublishing.com
rothwellpublishing@bigpond.com
Tele: 61 3 5966 5628

First Published 2007,reprinted 2010

Typeset by Artastic Images
Printed in China by Everbest Printing Co. Ltd

National Library of Australia Cataloguing-in-Publication data:

Rothwell, Jo, 1962-.
My Great Ocean Road Adventure.
For Children
ISBN 978 0 9757230 4 3 (pbk.)

1. Great Ocean Road (Vic) - Juvenile fiction. I. Rothwell, Bryce, 1966-. II. Title.

A823.4

My Great Ocean Road Adventure

Jo Rothwell
Illustrated by
Bryce Rothwell

Dear Mac and Pa,
I hope you are well.
I am writing to you with so much to tell.
We had an adventure, Nelly and me,
Along the Great Ocean Road....read on and you'll see.

EAN ROAD
WARBURTON PRIMARY SCHOOL
SCHOOL BUS

Our adventure began on the shores at Geelong,
When I spied an old bottle just bobbing along.
Well to my surprise, rolled up inside,
Was a crumpled up letter that was perfectly dry.

'Hello, name is Sally
and I'm writing you this note,
To find out if this message bottle
is capable to float.
They opened this
Great Ocean Road
in 1932,
And I think you should drive the
bends and check out all the views.
And if you feel inclined,
come and stop and say G'day,
And return my message bottle
when you travel down this way.

Yours Truly,
Sally

So of course we decided to return Sally's note,
And tell her indeed her bottle could float!
But where could we find her? Which way would we go?
Who could we ask who would most likely know?

Well an odd thing then happened; as odd things often do,
When a Ship Captain Bollard said, "Let me help you.
I'll come in your car; you can give me a lift,
And we'll go and ask Arthur who lives at Queenscliff."

Well it was a bit of a SQUASH but onward we went,
To return the old bottle and the note Sally sent.

Arthur T Middleton was a train on the track,
There was steam in his funnel; he was shiny and black.
He whistled that he knew where we needed to go,
To chat to a surfer who would certainly know.

He said, "I'll come in your car and we'll drive down the coast,
And stop when Bells Beach is on the signpost."

Well it was a bit of a SQUEEZE but onward we went,
To return the old bottle and the note Sally sent.

We stopped at Bells Beach; just next to Torquay,
And I leapt into the surf and paddled out to sea.
I balanced on my board and rode the biggest wave,
Right beside a surfing dude who said his name was Dave.
He said to me, "Drive further on, then journey up the hill,
And go to Erskine Falls to locate Ranger Jill."

Surfer Dave had the time to come along with us,
So he jumped into our car with a minimum of fuss.

Well it got a bit CRAMPED but onward we went,
To return the old bottle and the note Sally sent.

Past Anglesea and Lorne, then up to Erskine Falls,
Where the ferns were very green and the trees were very tall.
Ranger Jill told us the news that Sally had passed this way,
She journeyed further down the coast to the town Apollo Bay.

She said she knew the way to go; so move over Arthur T,
Jill jumped aboard our crowded car and sat right next to me.

Well it was a bit of a **CRUSH** but onward we went,
To return the old bottle and the note Sally sent.

Apollo Bay was all abuzz with people on holiday.
In the street a Seal named Pete had something new to say.
He said the Otway Lighthouse Keeper would definitely know,
About our message bottle and which way we had to go.

He said, "It would be no trouble to come along in your car,
Then you'd know precisely and exactly where you are."

Well it got a bit CROWDED but onward we went,
To return the old bottle and the note Sally sent.

So we found the Otway Lighthouse and saw the magic view,
And asked the Lighthouse Keeper if it was Sally that he knew.
He said, "I do recall a Sally who was here… then went on by,
She went to locate Rex, at the famous Otway Fly."

"Just in case you should get lost, I'll come along with you,
I'll take my trusty telescope as all good Keepers do."

Well it was a bit of a JAM but onward we went,
To return the old bottle and the note Sally sent.

We walked along the Otway Fly high up in the trees,
Where dinosaurs once roamed the land as far as you could see.
I was climbing up the tower when Rex popped up his head,
"I heard you are looking for Sally", Rex the dinosaur said.

"I know the way, I'll come with you, I'll squeeze into your car,
It's just around the corner; it really isn't far."

Well it was a bit of a SQUISH but onward we went,
To return the old bottle and the note Sally sent.

As we drove around the corner that wasn't really far,
I heard a little rattle from our crowded motorcar.
She said she was quite tired.... and then gave a little sigh,
She said a nap would do her good.... so stopped and shut her eyes.

It was here the Twelve Apostles stood proud and tall and straight.
There may have once been twelve......but I counted only eight!

In the sea beyond the rocks, a Whale swam up to play.
He told us he knew Sally and would help us find our way.
I hoped that Whale would **NOT** suggest to join us in our car,
Because that would be ridiculous; don't you think so Mac and Pa?

He said, "Follow along this shipwreck coast and learn about the fate,
Of the famous Loch Ard shipwreck in 1878........"

So we SQUEEZED back into Car; who had woken up at last,
And followed Whale down the coast to learn about the past.

To Loch Ard Gorge...............

............and London Bridge; where the arch had fallen down,
Past the Bay of Islands, and through the coastal towns.

Whale led us to Warrnambool to visit Flagstaff Hill,
Where history comes alive and time is standing still.
The school Ma'am said, "How do you do? I'll help you on your quest,
I need to travel in your car and guide you further west."

Still we were SQUASHED but onward we went,
To return the old bottle and the note Sally sent.

The school Ma'am said 'Port Fairy' was where to stop the car,
And ask the fisherman on the boat which is called the Western Star.
He said, "I know Sally very well; she was here just yesterday,
Let me come along with you and I'll direct you on the way."

And so **FINALLY** we found Sally.....

..................and joined the lengthy queue,
Of folks returning bottles coloured green and coloured blue.

And I really think that Sally will know the answer to her note,
That her message in a bottle can **DEFINITELY** float!

Now our quest was over, we turned our car around,
To farewell all our friends as we headed homeward bound.

One by one we said goodbye; it was sad to see them go.

The car ride got less SQUISHY .....and we had to have it towed!

Our Great Ocean Road adventure is now at an end,
And so is this letter that I'll soon have to send.
I know we'll return, we will often come back,
And you can come too, Pa and Mac.

Love Always
Harry XXX

Queenscliff is a great place because there is a steam train and a fort place and a ferry that goes to Sorrento. There is also a horse and cart and Mummy loves to shop there.

Building the Great Ocean Road

Well Mac and Pa, this road was built ages ago and was opened in 1932. Not sure if you remember that? Anyway, lots and lots of blokes that returned from the war helped out. Mummy said there were about 3000 workers. Wow! I am glad that I wasn't around then because it is a really long way to dig with a shovel. I used my shovel in my sandpit and dug a tunnel and that took me all day and hurt my hand.

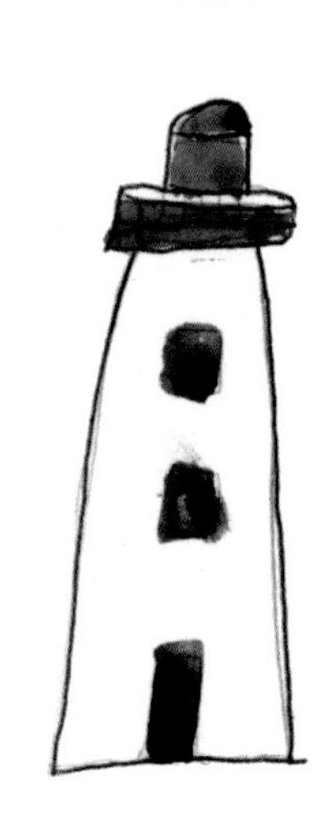

Otway Lighthouse

I bet you didn't know that this lightho is the oldest lighthouse on mainla Australia? Daddy read that to me wl we were there. He also read that it star operating in 1848. Seems to me that l of stuff around here happened a long ti ago.

There are lots of other lighthouses alc the Great Ocean Road. I really liked one at Aireys Inlet called Split Po because I thought it was called Spit Po and that would be a bit funny...and a yucky!

Twelve Apostles

These are the giant bits of rock that stick up out of the ocean. Mummy said this happened because lots and lots of water over millions of years has crashed into the limestone cliffs and bits have broken off. She said that they used to be called 'Sow and Piglets' which is just really funny. I reckon if I were a Mummy pig or a piglet, I wouldn't be climbing around on these rocks, I would be at home watching Playschool.

Shipwreck Coast

I just cannot believe how many unluc ships have crashed around here. Mumr said there were over 700 and one of t famous ones was the Loch Ard. We we to learn all about this at the Museum a saw the ceramic peacock that was fou from this boat. It must have been packed lots of bubble wrap because it was harc damaged. I just love that bubble wrap stu because you can sit and pop the bubbles day. Mummy said that they would ha most likely used straw to pack the peacoc Oh well!

The Otways

This is a big place with lots of trees and koalas and there are even glow worms! Lots of people come to do walks. We walked down to the Otway Fly where there are pathways made up in the treetops. I climbed up the tower with Daddy but Mummy said she would stay down to take our photo. Not sure if you were around when the dinosaurs were here Mac and Pa, but gee that would have been just great to see!

Portland

Well I know that in the Mornington Peninsula book told you that Sorrento was the first place Europe people settled in Victoria in 1803 ...well apparent Portland was Victoria's first permanent settlement 1834. I guess this means that they came to stay.

Port Fairy

This is a place with lots of fishing boats and Dadc said they have this really great music festival eve year. I wanted to know where all the fairies an elves lived. Mummy said that Port Fairy was mo likely named after a boat. This is very confusing.

Beaches

I just cannot believe how many beaches there are along the Great Ocean Road. I will try and list them for you alphabetically, but I really think you should just come here and find them for yourselves. There is Anglesea and Apollo Bay and Bancoora and Barwon Heads and Bells Beach and Bridgewater Bay and Eastern Beach and Fairhaven and Jan Juc (crazy name) and Johanna and Kennett River (both river and beach!) and Lorne and Ocean Grove and Point Lonsdale and Point Roadknight and Port Campbell and Port Fairy and Portland and Queenscliff and Torquay and Warrnambool and Wye River (another river) and 13th Beach. Not sure where to put 13th Beach in the alphabet. I must admit Mummy helped me sort this list.

Warrnambool

Warrnambool has this great place called Logans Beach, where you can go and look for whales. WOW! Mummy thought this was a great idea to stand on the land and look for whales. I think this is because last time we went looking for whales, we were in a boat and she got really really sick.

Geelong Bollards

I would really like to have a fe bollards at my home. Daddy sai that they use bollards to tie boat up to so they do not float away These bollards in Geelong are nc used for boats though. Someon clever has found old bollards an made them into people. Ther are more than 100 of them i Geelong. I drew you this one of lifesaver. Daddy thought it was pirate. Silly Daddy.. Doesn't h know that pirates have an ey patch?